Karen's Unicorn

Little Sister

Karen's Unicorn
Ann M. Martin

Illustrations by Susan Tang

A
LITTLE APPLE
PAPERBACK

SCHOLASTIC INC.
New York Toronto London Auckland Sydney

The author gratefully acknowledges
Gabrielle Charbonnet
for her help
with this book.

ISBN 0-590-06587-4

Copyright © 1997 by Ann M. Martin. All rights reserved. Published by Scholastic Inc. BABY-SITTERS LITTLE SISTER and LITTLE APPLE PAPER-BACKS are trademarks and/or registered trademarks of Scholastic Inc.

10 9 8 7 6 5 4 3 2   7 8 9/9 0 1/0 2/0

Printed in the U.S.A.   40
First Scholastic printing, September 1997

Princess Karenna

Just then Princess Rosamund heard a noise. She peered out from behind a tree. There in the clearing stood . . . a unicorn.

A tingle went down my spine! It was a September afternoon. I was reading the greatest book ever: *The Unicorn's Magic*. I love unicorns!

Not long ago I saw a TV show called *Do They Exist?* It was all about creatures such as the Loch Ness Monster, The Abominable Snowman, dragons, mermaids, and unicorns. I am not sure about the others, but I *know* unicorns are real. No one has seen a unicorn for a long time, but that does not mean anything.

Since then I have read all about unicorns. They are special, wonderful, magical animals. A unicorn is a lot like a horse, but right in the middle of its forehead is one horn.

I turned over on my bed and plumped my pillows. I had been telling all my friends about unicorns. So far no one believed in them but me. That did not bother me.

I had even told my two families about unicorns. (I will explain about my two families in a minute.) Everyone thought unicorns were interesting, but nobody thought they were real.

Here are some unicorn facts:

1) They are always pure white.

2) They are hard to find. (They are very shy.)

3) Their horns are magical. If you want to drink from a stream in the woods, and a unicorn comes along and puts its horn into

the stream, then the water will be safe to drink. I am not making that up.

4) If you see a unicorn, you can make a wish. Sometimes your wish will come true.

5) You can make friends with them only if you are very, very good. They are picky.

So you can see how magical and special they are. Reading about unicorns made me wish that I were Princess Karenna. (Usually I am very glad just to be me.) My name is Karen Brewer. I am seven years old. I am in Ms. Colman's second-grade class at Stoneybrook Academy.

If I were Princess Karenna, I would be gigundoly beautiful. I would wear long, fancy dresses. I would have my own castle in the woods. And I could go out in the woods and try to make friends with a unicorn. I would be very, very, very good.

If I were Princess Karenna, I would sit quietly in the forest. Maybe I would sing a nice song. Then a unicorn would hear the song and come to meet me. I could pat him and he could rest his head in my lap. (I bet their horns are heavy.) Then I would be the only person in the world with her very own unicorn. I could make a daisy-chain necklace for the unicorn. And I could make wishes.

Everyone would ask to see my unicorn, but I would keep him secret. Maybe someone would even write a book about me: *Princess Karenna and Her Magical Secret Unicorn.* And then I would be famous. But still I would not tell —

Knock, knock.

I jumped. "Who is it?" I called.

The door opened. "It is me, Andrew," said my little brother. "I need your help."

Andrew's Bicycle

"There is still daylight left before dinnertime," said Andrew. "Could you please come help me with the bike?"

I sighed and put a bookmark in my book. I took off my blue glasses and put on my pink glasses. (My blue glasses are just for reading.)

I am a big sister, which means I help Andrew with many things. (I even taught him how to read.) Usually I like helping Andrew. It is important to be a good big sister. But lately Andrew wanted my help with riding a two-wheeled bicycle. And it was very hard on both of us.

"Andrew," I said. "You are only four years old, going on five. That is very young to ride a two-wheeler. No one I know rode a two-wheeler when they were four going on five."

"I can do it," said Andrew. "I want to be like the big kids."

"I was six going on seven when I learned to ride a two-wheeler," I said. "It is not easy."

Andrew looked very disappointed. "Plee-ease?" he said. "I am all ready." He was wearing his bicycle helmet, and elbow and knee guards. He looked like a hockey player.

"Well, okay," I said. "But I think it would be better to stick with your tricycle for awhile longer."

Andrew frowned. "Tricycles are for ba-bies!" he said. "I am not a baby."

We went outside. It was almost autumn. Soon all the leaves would start turning colors. That is my favorite thing about fall.

Andrew wheeled the bike out of our garage. It was my old bike. I am too big for it now. It was small and red, and had fat tires and some rust on the handlebars. It was too small for me, but it was still too big for Andrew.

"Maybe Seth could put training wheels on this bike," I said.

"Training wheels are for babies!" said Andrew. "Like Emily Michelle."

Before I tell you who Emily Michelle is, I better explain about my two families. That way you will not be confused. Andrew and I were at the little house this month, with our little-house family. Next month we would be back at the big house, with our big-house family.

A long time ago, Andrew and I used to live at the big house all the time, with Mommy, Daddy, and our cranky cat, Boo-Boo. Then Mommy and Daddy decided to get a divorce. So Andrew and I moved with Mommy to the little house.

Pretty soon Mommy met Seth Engle, and they got married. So Seth is my stepfather. (He is gigundoly nice.) He has two pets — a cat, Rocky, and a dog, Midgie. They are the people and pets in my little-house family.

Daddy also got married again, to Elizabeth. She already had four children. (She was married once before too.) David Michael is seven, like me. He goes to Stoneybrook Elementary. Kristy is thirteen. She is the best stepsister in the whole world. Sam and Charlie go to high school, because they are very old. Emily Michelle does not go to school at all. She is two and a half. (That is why Andrew said she was a baby.) Daddy and Elizabeth adopted Emily Michelle from a country called Vietnam. Finally, Nannie, who is Elizabeth's mother, came to live at the big house to help take care of all the people and pets. Nannie is my stepgrandmother. Besides Boo-Boo, the other pets are David Michael's gigundo puppy named Shannon and Andrew's and my goldfish that stay at Daddy's house. Plus we have two pets who travel back and forth with us: my pet rat, Emily Junior (I named her after Emily Michelle), and Bob, Andrew's hermit crab. So that is my big-house family. The big house is always very exciting!

Now Andrew and I stay at the little house for a month, and at the big house for a month. It is a good solution. Since Andrew and I have two of so many things (one at each house), I made up nicknames for us: I call us Andrew Two-Two and Karen Two-Two. We have two houses, two cats, and two dogs. I even have two bicycles and Andrew has two tricycles (which he would not ride anymore). I even have two pairs of glasses, and two best friends, and two stuffed cats, and two pieces of Tickly, my special blanket. Most of the time it is fun to be a two-two.

Now Andrew climbed onto my old red bike. "Okay, start pedaling," I told Andrew. "It is easier to balance when you go faster." (I do not know why that is, but it is true.)

"I am trying," said Andrew. His feet could hardly reach the pedals. I had to hold the bike up with both hands. I trotted down the sidewalk as he pedaled. But he still fell, even though I tried hard not to let him.

By the time Mommy called us for dinner, I was tired and hot and dirty. Whew, I thought. It is a good thing I have only *one* little brother!

Seth's Problem

"And I have a bruise on my shin and one on my shoulder," said Andrew.

"Hmm," said Mommy. "Andrew, maybe you are just too young to ride a two-wheeler." She scooped some potatoes onto his plate.

"No, I am not," said Andrew stubbornly. "My bruises do not hurt *too* much."

"Goody, fried chicken," I said. "May I have a leg, please?"

Mommy put a leg on my plate. Legs are

very easy to eat. I picked mine up and took a bite.

"Did someone feed Midgie?" asked Mommy.

"I did," I said. "One big scoop of kibble."

"Thank you, honey," said Mommy.

I smiled. If I were Princess Karenna, I bet I would be so good that a unicorn would come to me right away.

"Seth, may I have the bread, please?" I asked politely.

Seth had not said much since he had gotten home from work. He is a carpenter. He makes very beautiful furniture out of wood. He has his own workshop downtown.

He cut off a bite of chicken and ate it. He did not look up.

"Um, Seth?" I asked. "May I have the bread?"

He did not seem to hear me. Mommy reached for the bread and passed it to me. Then she put her hand on Seth's shoulder. He jumped.

"Everything okay?" Mommy asked.

"I am sorry," said Seth. "I have something on my mind. Today my landlord told me that he wants to take over the whole building where my shop is. That means I cannot rent the space for my shop anymore. And *that* means I will not have any place to work in."

"Oh, dear," said Mommy.

"He is going to improve the building, then charge more rent," said Seth.

"And we cannot afford the higher rent?" asked Mommy.

"No. I will need to find a new place for my shop," replied Seth. "I need to move."

My eyebrows rose. Moving Seth's shop would be a very, very, very hard job. He has about a million pieces of wood there. Plus tons of big machines.

"I am worried about finding a new place," said Seth. "I did not mean to ignore you, Karen."

"It is okay," I said. "Do not worry about moving. We will all help you."

Andrew nodded and ate another green bean.

"When will you have to move?" asked Mommy.

"In about six weeks," said Seth. "That is not very much time. I have been at this shop for ten years now. Tomorrow I will start looking for a new place to rent."

"Why don't you move into our garage?" I said. "We can park the cars on the street."

Seth smiled. "I am afraid the garage is not big enough."

"You could ask the landlord to change his mind," said Andrew.

"I do not think that would work either," said Seth. "But thank you for your suggestions. Mommy and I will have to talk about it and come up with a solution. Everything will work out for the best, I am sure."

The Circus Is Coming!

When I am at the little house, Nancy Dawes and I ride the school bus together to Stoneybrook Academy. Nancy is one of my two best friends. She lives next door to the little house. Hannie Papadakis is my other best friend. She lives across the street and one house down from the big house. Nancy and Hannie and I call ourselves the Three Musketeers, because we always try to stick together. Through thick and thin.

Today Nancy and I shared a seat and looked out the bus window.

"Look at that maple tree!" said Nancy. "Its leaves are starting to change."

I nodded. "Soon it will be really and truly fall. Then we will have Halloween. Then Thanksgiving. Then Christmas. Hooray!" I love autumn. It is the start of all the holidays.

"Well, soon *I* will have Rosh Hashanah," said Nancy. Nancy's family celebrates Jewish holidays. "Then Yom Kippur. Then Sukkot. Then Thanksgiving. Then Hanukkah. Yippee!"

Our bus stopped at a stoplight. Suddenly, I grabbed Nancy's arm. "Nancy!" I cried. "Look at that!"

On a building at the corner were several posters. On one poster was a big picture of a clown. It said:

Come One, Come All,
to the Fabulous Circus DeMarco!
Featuring Our Extra-Special Attraction:
A Real, Live UNICORN!

I gasped. "A unicorn!" I said. "Do you see that? The circus is coming, and it has a real unicorn in it!"

At school on the playground everyone was talking about the circus.

"My mom said we could go as soon as it opens," said Omar Harris.

"I want to go this weekend," said Sara Ford.

"I am sure I will go the first day," said Pamela Harding.

I looked at Nancy and rolled my eyes. Pamela Harding is my best enemy. She can be kind of snobby.

"Did you see the signs for the circus?" cried Hannie, running to Nancy and me.

"Let's try to go together, the Three Mus keteers," said Nancy. "We will all ask our parents tonight."

"Yes," I said. "I cannot wait to see a real, live unicorn. This is the greatest thing that has ever happened in Stoneybrook."

* * *

After the bell rang, we went into our classroom. Ms. Colman, the best teacher in the whole world, was there.

"Attention, class," she said. "I think I can guess what you all are excited about."

"The circus!" I cried. (I forgot to raise my hand.) "The unicorn!"

Ms. Colman smiled. She is gigundoly nice. She almost never yells. But sometimes she has to ask me to use my indoor voice or to simmer down.

"We will talk about the circus after Terri takes attendance," said Ms. Colman. Terri Barkan is a twin. Her sister, Tammy, is in our class too.

Boo and bullfrogs, I thought. I love taking attendance. It is a very important job.

When Terri was finished, Ms. Colman stood at the front of our classroom. "I know you have just found out about the circus. So I thought it would be interesting to talk about circuses for a few minutes before we start our regular work."

I raised my hand and waved it around. I

sit in the very front row, where Ms. Colman can see me. My pretend husband, Ricky Torres, sits next to me. We are in the first row because we are glasses-wearers. Ms. Colman is a glasses-wearer too.

"Yes, Karen?" said Ms. Colman.

"There will be a real, live unicorn at the circus," I said. "The posters said so!"

From the row behind me, Bobby Gianelli (a sometimes bully) snorted. "It is not a real unicorn," he said. "They do not exist. It is fake."

"The poster said *real, live unicorn*," I pointed out. Sometimes boys think they know everything.

Ms. Colman held up her hand for silence. "I want to talk about circuses in general," she said. "Did you know circuses have been around for hundreds of years? They grew out of the tradition of traveling shows. Early circuses featured jugglers, acrobats, singers, and any unusual act people could think of. The circus would travel around the country-side, entertaining people. Instead of buying tickets, people would throw the performers coins or food or whatever they had. It is only recently that circuses have become organized, and had tents, and sold tickets."

"I saw a huge circus at Madison Square Garden in New York City," said Jannie Gilbert. She is one of Pamela Harding's best friends. "They had things going on in three rings, all at the same time. I saw performing dogs and horses and a man on a motorcycle riding on a tightrope."

"The circus in town now, the Circus De-Marco, is much smaller than that," explained Ms. Colman. "They have only one tent. They have fewer acts. And they have no animal acts."

"Except the unicorn," I pointed out.

"There is no unicorn!" said Bobby.

I crossed my arms over my chest. "It *says* so right on the *poster*."

"Okay, class," said Ms. Colman. "We will talk about the circus again another time. Now let's take out our spelling books."

Ms. Colman's Surprising
Announcement

"**W**hat are you going to wish for when you see the unicorn?" I asked Hannie and Nancy. It was Friday morning before school. I was sitting with them in the back row of Ms. Colman's class. Before I got my glasses, the Three Musketeers all sat together.

"Um, well . . ." said Hannie. She glanced at Nancy.

"The thing is, Karen," said Nancy, "I do not really believe in unicorns."

"Even though there is one on the circus poster?"

"Yes," said Hannie. "I asked my daddy, and he said unicorns are a nice story, but they do not really exist. He said the circus was just pretending to have a unicorn to make people happy. I am sorry."

"That is what my mommy said too," added Nancy. "And I believe her."

"Hmm," I said. "On television they said that no one had ever *proved* that unicorns do *not* exist."

Hannie shrugged.

Just then Ms. Colman came in. I sat down at my own desk. After Natalie Springer took attendance, Ms. Colman said my four favorite words: "I have an announcement."

Hooray! I thought. I love Ms. Colman's announcements. They add excitement to my day.

"Our class will be going on a field trip next Tuesday," Ms. Colman said. "To . . . the circus!"

"Yes!" I cried, jumping up in my seat.

"Karen, please simmer down," said Ms. Colman.

24

I sat down again and put my hand over my mouth so I would not yell anything. I was *so* excited. I had been asking Mommy about going to the circus, but she had not agreed yet.

"Please have your parents sign these permission slips. Return them on Monday. In addition," Ms. Colman went on, "you will have a special assignment to work on at the circus. You must find three things that could have been the same in a circus one hundred years ago, and three things that are different."

It was very hard for me to sit still.

"Our trip will also include a behind-the-scenes tour of the circus and a close-up look at their unicorn," said Ms. Colman with a smile. "So you will be able to decide for yourselves whether it is real or not."

"Will we be close enough to see the masking tape holding the horn to its head?" asked Bobby Gianelli. Several kids in class laughed.

That did not bother me. I turned around

in my chair and grinned at Hannie and Nancy. They smiled back. Next Tuesday we would see the unicorn. And then everyone would know that I was right!

"The first-, second-, and third-graders are going," I told my little-house family at dinner that night. "I cannot wait. I have already been thinking about what to wear."

Dinnertime is when my family shares special news and events. Tonight I was trying to share, but only Andrew was listening. Mommy and Seth were quiet. Mommy gave me a smile, but I did not know if she had heard me.

"What is wrong?" I asked.

Mommy sighed. "Seth and I have been looking for a new workshop space. It is very hard to find." (Mommy helps Seth in his shop.)

"Why is it hard?" asked Andrew.

"The places that are big enough are too expensive. The places we can afford are too small," explained Seth.

Andrew and I looked at each other. These were grown-up problems. I did not know how to fix them. I do not like it when Mommy and Seth have grown-up problems. I like it when everything is fine.

"I could work longer hours to make more money to pay more rent," said Seth. He and Mommy both looked unhappy at that idea.

"You already work very hard," said Mommy.

"I could take on some refinishing projects," said Seth. "They pay well."

"You would not be very happy doing that," said Mommy.

I sighed and pushed my carrots around on my plate. I wanted to talk about the circus. I wanted to talk about the unicorn. I decided that after dinner I would read to Andrew about unicorns.

The Wishing Plan

"Do not let go!" cried Andrew. He was pedaling hard. I ran behind him down the sidewalk, holding on to the rack over the back tire.

"I cannot keep up!" I said. "Just pedal!"

Andrew turned his head to see if I was still there.

"Do not turn around!" I yelled. But it was too late. *Crash!* That was the second time this morning that Andrew had plowed headfirst into our neighbor's hedge. I helped him haul the bike out of the bush.

We flopped down on the grass, breathing hard.

"Andrew," I said. "This is just not a good idea."

"Yes it is," insisted Andrew. "I am getting better."

"Why don't we go inside and watch Saturday-morning cartoons?" I said. "It is almost time for *Boom-Boom the Wonder Cat*."

"I do not want to watch cartoons," said Andrew. "Besides, Mommy will say it is too pretty outside to be inside watching TV."

Andrew had a point. Mommy and Seth do not like TV that much. And it *was* very pretty outside. I sat up. So far this morning Andrew had crashed into the hedge twice, into a tree once (he had cried that time), and into the big pile of leaves that Mr. Dawes had raked up on his front lawn. Mr. Dawes had not been very happy about having to rake up the leaves again.

But still Andrew would not give up. Everyone said he was too young and too little to ride a two-wheeler, but he did not believe them. On our street were a bunch of other kids. Bobby Gianelli lived close by. His little sister, Alicia, was four, just like Andrew. She still rode a tricycle. Willie Barnes was five years old. He rode a tricycle (a big black one).

"Why don't we paint your tricycle black?" I suggested. "Then it will look very powerful."

"Tricycles are for babies!" Andrew said. He stood up. He picked up the bicycle. I thought, Here we go again.

After lunch, I went to my room to think. I had a lot to think about. Right now, no one in my little-house family was very happy. (Except me.) Andrew was trying too hard to ride a two-wheeler. Mommy and Seth were worried about the workshop. I decided we all needed help.

Where would we get help? From the magical, wonderful unicorn, of course! In just three days I would see a real, live unicorn. I would even see it up close. I knew that if I made wishes while I was very close to the unicorn, my wishes would probably be granted. It was a great idea!

I sat down at my desk and made a list. Some wishes were for my family. Some were for me.

UNICORN WISH LIST

1. I WISH TO SEE THE UNICORN TWICE.

2. I WISH THAT ANDREW WILL EITHER LEARN HOW TO RIDE A TWO-WHEELER OR GIVE UP ON THE IDEA.

3. I WISH I WOULD GET A LETTER FROM MAXIE. (MAXIE MEDVIN IS MY PEN-PAL FRIEND IN NEW YORK CITY. I LOVE GETTING HER LETTERS.)

4. I WISH TO DO WELL ON MY NEXT MATH TEST.

5. I WISH THAT SETH'S WORKSHOP PROBLEM WILL BE SOLVED.

I felt much better when I had finished my list. I knew once the unicorn got to work on my wishes, everything would be better.

That night at dinner I tapped my fork against my glass.

"Attention, everyone, please," I said. "I

just want to announce that all of our problems will be taken care of next week."

"What problems?" asked Andrew.

"Your bike riding," I told him. "And Seth's workshop. When I see the unicorn at the circus on Tuesday, I am going to wish for these problems to be solved. So you see, you have nothing to worry about. Next week everything will be fine again. We will not have to worry anymore. The unicorn will fix everything."

"Oh, great!" Andrew said happily. "That is good news. Thank you, Karen."

"No problem," I said. I munched on a celery stick. Mommy and Seth nodded and smiled. They did not look one hundred percent convinced. I knew they did not really believe in the unicorn. But I did. And that was what was important.

Circus DeMarco

On Tuesday morning I chose my clothes carefully. This is what I wore for our circus field trip: my new jeans, my pink-and-white unicorn sweatshirt, my pink socks, and my white sneakers. I pulled my hair into a ponytail and tied it with a pink-and-white scrunchie. Last, I stuck my list of wishes into my pocket. I hoped the unicorn would like my sweatshirt. I hoped he would be able to tell that I really believed in him.

At school, three yellow buses waited for us. Nancy and I decided to be partners, and

Hannie was going to be Natalie Springer's partner.

I could hardly sit still. After we had been on the bus for awhile, Nancy said, "Karen, please quit bouncing. You are going to make me bus-sick." After that I tried to sit quietly.

The Circus DeMarco was at the Old Fairgrounds. When we arrived, we saw a huge green-and-yellow striped tent. Two smaller tents were off to the side. Inside the big tent we had great seats, right in the second row. (The first-graders sat in the first row.)

I was so excited I had to hop all the way into the tent and down the aisle to our seats. When the lights dimmed and the ringmaster came out, I grabbed Nancy's hand and squeezed it. She smiled at me.

You have probably been to a circus before, so I do not have to describe *every*thing. But I will tell you some things. First we saw a man and a woman and a little boy who could bend themselves into pretzels. Then we saw two girls on the trapeze. I thought they were going to fall a bunch of times, but they did not. Then a man and a woman walked on the tightrope and jumped up and down on it. They held little umbrellas.

Nancy, Hannie, Natalie, and I shared a large popcorn and a bag of peanuts.

We saw clowns who did acrobatic stunts, and a strong man who could lift practically anything (even a heavy trunk full of bricks).

I loved seeing all the acts, but what I really wanted to see was the unicorn.

After the strong man's act, the circus tent suddenly went dark. Everyone was very quiet. Out of the darkness came the ringmaster's voice.

"And now, ladies, gentlemen, and kids of all ages," he said, "comes the moment you've been waiting for. Long believed extinct or mythical, the unicorn is rarely seen by mere mortals. It is our great privilege to bring to you the unicorn of the Circus DeMarco!"

I clapped as hard as I could. One spotlight shone at the back of the tent. Sparkly glitter swirled down from the ceiling like magical snow.

I gasped. "The unicorn!"

A beautiful, pure-white unicorn stepped slowly into the spotlight. On its forehead was a long, straight horn with a bit of a spiral, like soft ice cream. Its white mane and tail looked silky. It wore a fancy jeweled bridle on its head and a shiny sequined blanket, but no reins or saddle. The sparkly glitter shone all around it, and the spotlight gleamed. The unicorn looked as if it were made out of a magical moonbeam. It was the most gigundoly beautiful thing I had ever seen.

The unicorn trotted slowly around the large ring. I almost made my wishes then. But I decided to wait until I saw it up close. Into the ring stepped a beautiful maiden with long, dark hair. She wore a white princess dress and carried a magic wand. (I did not really think it was magic. Just the unicorn.)

She tapped the unicorn with the pretend magic wand, and the unicorn bent down on one knee. It touched its horn to the ground.

Then the ringmaster came out again.

"We are pleased to offer you the once-in-a-lifetime chance to ask our unicorn some questions," he said. "As you know, a unicorn cannot lie. But you must keep your questions simple, with yes-or-no answers."

I did not wait to raise my hand. I leaped up and shouted, "Are you real?"

The maiden looked at the unicorn. Then the unicorn nodded its head! It actually nodded up and down, to say yes!

I sat down and fanned myself with my program. Take that, Bobby Gianelli, I thought.

My Wishes

Several more people asked the unicorn questions. It answered yes or no by nodding or shaking its head. Then the beautiful maiden led it out of the ring, and the circus was over.

But not our field trip. Next we would go on our behind-the-scenes tour.

"Wasn't that the most gigundoly beautiful thing you have ever seen?" I asked Hannie and Nancy.

"It *was* really pretty," said Hannie.

"It looked very real," said Nancy.

"I wonder how they got that horn to stick on," said Natalie.

I sighed. Some people cannot believe what they see right in front of their very eyes.

We waited with Ms. Colman and our parent helpers until the ringmaster came to get us. He was very tall. He had a big mustache that twirled out to the sides.

"Welcome!" he said with a smile. "Are you ready for a close-up look at circus life?"

"Yes!" we shouted. And a close-up look at the unicorn, I thought.

The ringmaster took us out of the large tent and led us to a bunch of trucks and campers. I looked around for the unicorn, but I did not see it.

To tell you the truth, I was not too interested in the rest of the tour. I already knew a lot about circuses because I had gone to circus camp one summer. So I knew that the performers live in trailers, and that the circus kids have tutors and do not go to regular school.

40

I was about to burst when the ringmaster finally said, "And now, who wants to see our unicorn?"

"I do! I do!" I yelled, jumping up and down.

"Karen," said Ms. Colman. She meant I had to mind my manners.

One of the smaller tents was a souvenir stand, where you could buy programs and toys and food and neat things. The other tent was just for the circus performers. It was where they changed costumes and rested between acts. One part of it was roped off. Several bales of hay made a low wall. And there, munching on some hay, was the unicorn.

Even without the spotlight and the glitter, it was very, very beautiful. It was not wearing its fancy show costume anymore. Its white coat gleamed. Its large brown eyes looked very smart and wise. It had "magic" written all over it.

When we got closer (we had to stay behind the rope), I felt as if I could hardly

breathe. This was one of the very few unicorns anywhere in the world. Hardly anyone ever got to see one, and here I was, only a few feet away. I could not believe it.

The lovely maiden had changed into a blue running suit and put her long hair into a braid held with a rubber band. She stood next to the unicorn, with her hand on its back.

"The unicorn is so, so beautiful," I said. "Is it a he?"

"Yes, he's a boy," said the trainer.

"Does he have a name?" I asked.

"He has a special, secret unicorn name," said the trainer. "But we call him Bob."

Bob did not seem like a very special name for one of the most magical creatures on earth, but I did not say so.

"How do you get the horn to stay on?" asked Bobby Gianelli loudly. "Superglue?"

The trainer smiled. "Look at how long and heavy his horn is," she said. "Do you really think superglue would work?"

Bobby frowned. "Is it taped on?"

"Do you see any tape?" The trainer put out her hand and ruffled the unicorn's mane with her fingers. There was no tape anywhere around the horn.

"See, Bobby?" I said. "He is real. You have to face facts."

Bobby frowned harder. "He is not real. I know he is not."

"Okay, everyone," said Ms. Colman. "It is time to go now."

Suddenly I remembered my wish list. I put my hand in my pocket and held my list, but I did not need to look at it. Quickly I whispered my wishes to myself, while I looked into the unicorn's eyes. Neither of us blinked. As soon as I made my wishes, he lowered his head and took another bite of hay.

"Thank you," I whispered.

Do Not Worry

Before we got back on our school buses, Ms. Colman let us go to the souvenir tent for ten minutes. Nancy bought a photo album of the circus performers. Hannie bought a tiny flashlight with a clown's face on it. Its red nose glowed when she turned it on. I bought a silver necklace with a small unicorn charm on it.

"I will wear this until all my wishes come true," I said, fastening it around my neck.

"What wishes?" asked Hannie.

I told the other two Musketeers about my

wish list. Hannie and Nancy looked at each other.

"Well, I really hope your wishes come true," said Hannie politely.

"Me too," said Nancy. "Let us know if we can help somehow."

"Thank you," I said. "But the unicorn will take care of everything."

When I got home that afternoon, Mommy and Andrew were in the kitchen. Mommy fixed me a snack — a Rice Krispie treat and a glass of milk. Yum!

"I saw the unicorn today," I said. "I saw him up close, and he was one hundred percent real."

"Really? Gosh," said Andrew. (His preschool class was going to the circus the next day.)

"So I made all my wishes," I went on. "I looked him right in the eyes and made my wishes. So I guess we do not have to worry anymore."

"Goody," said Andrew. "Did you wish about my bike riding?"

"Yes," I said. "And about Seth's workshop, and a few other things. I bet the unicorn will get started on the wishes right away. But it might take a little while. We will have to be patient." I felt very grown-up, saying that.

"Please do not get your hopes up, Karen," said Mommy. "I am glad you had a good time at the circus. And I am glad you thought the unicorn looked real. But sometimes things are not what they seem."

I munched on my Rice Krispie treat. I did not mind Mommy saying that to me. Mommies are supposed to say things like that. But I knew the unicorn was real, and that our troubles were over.

"May I be excused?" I asked. "I am finished."

In my room, I thought about the unicorn. Probably a lot of people had made wishes today. The unicorn might have hundreds of wishes to grant. It might take him awhile to get to mine, I thought. I decided that I would try to help him along.

First I checked my letter box. It is a shoe box that I decorated. In it I keep all the letters I get. When I looked through it, I realized that Maxie had written me three months ago. I could not remember if I had written back so I pulled out a postcard and addressed it to her.

DEAR MAXIE,

HOW ARE YOU? I AM FINE. TODAY I SAW A REAL UNICORN AT THE CIRCUS. HE WAS BEAUTIFUL. I WISH YOU COULD HAVE SEEN HIM. DOES THE CIRCUS COME TO NEW YORK? IF IT DOES, GO SEE IT.

LOVE, YOUR PEN PAL, KAREN

Then I stuck a stamp on it and put it by the front door to mail. I thought about another wish: to do well on my next math test. So I opened up my math book and did some practice problems.

I was glad that I was giving the unicorn a helping hand.

I was almost done when Andrew knocked on my door.

"Karen?" he called. "I am ready to ride the bike again. Can you help me?"

I closed my book and sat up. I crossed my fingers and closed my eyes for a second. I *really* hoped the unicorn had had a chance to work on the bike-riding wish.

Some Wishes Come True

"Hooray!" I cried. It was the next Thursday, and Ms. Colman had just handed back our math tests.

I showed Ricky my paper. "Only three wrong!"

"That is very good, Karen," he said. "I missed five." Ricky is a very nice pretend husband.

"Not only that," I said, "but this was one of my unicorn wishes. My wishes are coming true!"

"Do not start about the unicorn," said Ricky. "I asked my dad, and he said unicorns do not exist. My dad is never wrong."

"He is wrong this time," I said. "Because my wishes are coming true."

"Like what else?" asked Natalie Springer. (She is another glasses-wearer. She sits on the other side of me.)

"Like my pen pal in New York called me last night," I said proudly. "I wished for her to write me soon, but a phone call is even better. And that wish came true."

I had been very glad to hear from Maxie. I love getting phone calls. Especially long-distance ones. They are very special. (Not long ago, I got into trouble for using the phone too much. But I am allowed to use it again now.)

"If the Circus DeMarco unicorn is real," said Sara Ford, "where did they get it? Why isn't it more famous? Why aren't scientists studying it?"

"Yeah," said Ian Johnson. "If it was practically the only unicorn in the world, it would be worth a lot of money. It would not be in a small circus. It would be in a big zoo."

I shrugged. "All I know is that Bob is real," I said. "I do not know why or how. But you saw him yourselves."

No one looked convinced.

"Attention, people," said Ms. Colman. "Please save your conversations for after class. Right now I would like you to write two paragraphs about anything you like. Please write neatly and remember to put your name at the top of the paper. I will collect your papers in twenty minutes."

Hmm. I thought. Two paragraphs about anything I want?

UNICORNS
BY KAREN BREWER

UNICORNS ARE VERY SPECIAL, MAGICAL CREATURES. THEY ARE LIKE HORSES. BUT THEY HAVE A LONG HORN IN THE MIDDLE OF THEIR FOREHEADS. THEY ARE PURE WHITE. THEY ARE HARD TO FIND.

SOME PEOPLE DO NOT BELIEVE IN UNICORNS.

EVEN THOUGH THEY ARE STANDING RIGHT IN FRONT
OF ONE. BUT I BELIEVE IN UNICORNS, NO MATTER
WHAT ANYONE SAYS. I KNOW THEY ARE REAL. I
KNOW THEY GRANT WISHES. MAYBE SOMEDAY I
WILL HAVE MY OWN UNICORN.

Some Wishes Do Not Come True

The unicorn had done a good job on the math test and my phone call from Maxie. But he was being slow about my other wishes. I had wished for a chance to see the unicorn again. So far that had not come true. Mommy and Seth were too busy looking for a new workshop to take me to the circus. I could not go by myself.

And Seth had not found a new workshop. Every day Seth and Mommy checked the newspapers. They talked to people who rent buildings. They talked to their friends. They could not find a space that would work. At home it seemed as if all they talked about was the workshop. I was very tired of worrying about the workshop.

My last wish — that Andrew would either learn to ride a two-wheeler or give up — had not been granted yet either. On Friday afternoon Andrew put on his helmet and protective pads again. We went outside. It was cool and cloudy. Wind was blowing leaves off the trees. It looked very autumny. I wished I was inside watching TV with a cup of hot chocolate.

"Okay," said Andrew. "I am ready to get on."

I held the bike while he climbed up. Mommy had already lowered the seat and the handlebars as far as they would go. But it was still difficult for Andrew to reach the pedals.

"This time I want you to hold on the whole time," said Andrew.

"Andrew, I cannot," I said. "Once you start pedaling, I cannot run fast enough to keep up."

"I will pedal slowly."

"If you pedal slowly, it is harder to keep your balance," I said.

Andrew bit his lip, then nodded.

He stood up on the pedals and started pedaling. I trotted in back of him, holding him up. Soon he built up speed. He was not going gigundoly fast, but I had to let go. I hoped he would not notice.

"Pedal! Pedal!" I cried, running in back of him.

And he did! He pedaled hard. He was riding! He was riding a two-wheeler all by himself! But then he hit a crack in the sidewalk. He lost his balance. The bike tipped over, and Andrew fell and slid along the sidewalk. He and the bike slid right under our neighbor's bush.

"Andrew! Andrew! Are you all right?" I pulled the bike off of him. Then I helped Andrew sit up. His pants were torn from sliding on the sidewalk. His hand was scraped. He was about to cry.

"I am tired of crashing," he said. He sniffled and wiped his eyes. "I hate crashing."

"I do not blame you," I said, putting my arm around him. "It is scary to crash. But you are trying very hard." I waited a moment. "Andrew, do you think maybe — "

"No!" he said. "I know I can do this. I will never ride my tricycle again."

I just nodded. I know what it is like to have your heart set on something. All the same, I really, really hoped that Bob would do something about Andrew's bike-riding wish.

"There is a place over in Ryebrook," said Seth that night at dinner. "It is almost big enough. And the rent is about right."

"Ryebrook is almost forty-five minutes away," said Mommy. "We would have to leave early and come home late. We would have a very long commute."

I dipped a french fry in ketchup and ate it. This is what dinnertime sounded like every day now.

Seth sighed. "I know. But I do not know

what else to do. I cannot find anything in Stoneybrook."

Mommy sighed.

Andrew sighed.

I sighed. Bob, I thought, hurry up. We are depending on you.

Wishing Again

That night after dinner I lay on my bed with my feet propped against the wall. That is a good position to think in. I had a lot to think about.

It had been ten days since I made my wishes at the circus. I had tried to help Bob along. I had worn my special unicorn charm necklace all the time (even in the bathtub). I had truly believed.

But now I was worried. Only two wishes had come true. Ten days was plenty long enough for the other wishes. Even if Bob were really busy. What was I going to do?

I thought about how all the kids in Ms. Colman's class (even Hannie and Nancy) thought Bob was just a horse with a glued-on horn. Mommy and Seth probably thought so too. What if they were right? Then I shook my head. No. It was impossible. I had seen the unicorn with my own two eyes. He had been real, I could tell. He was not fake.

Maybe he just needed reminding. Maybe so many wishes had been wished at Bob that a few had gotten lost. I decided to make my wishes again. I closed my eyes and held my unicorn charm with both hands.

"Bob," I whispered, "I wish I knew your special secret unicorn name. But you know who you are. This is Karen Brewer, wishing again. My family needs your help. Please grant these wishes. One, I would like to see you again somehow. Two, please help Andrew with his bike. Three, please help Seth with his workshop. Thank you very much."

I lay with my eyes closed for a few more minutes, wishing hard. Then the phone rang, and I sat up. I heard Mommy answer the phone. I hoped it would be for me, but it was not. (A phone call would have cheered me up.)

"Oh, I see," I heard Mommy say. "Yes, I understand."

I opened the door to my room.

"Well, that would be very nice," said Mommy. "I am sure the kids would be thrilled. . . . Great. . . . Thank you." Then she hung up.

I poked my head out the door and looked at Mommy. She smiled at me.

"That was your father," she said. "He and Elizabeth were given some tickets to the circus for the big-house family. But now they can't use them. So he offered us four tickets for Sunday. Would you like that?"

"Yes!" I shouted, jumping up and down. "Yes!"

"That is what I thought," said Mommy. "It will be a nice treat for all of us."

I jumped up and down until Mommy asked me to simmer down. But I could not stop jumping completely. I would see the unicorn again. One more wish had come true!

Little-House Circus

On Sunday I wore my special unicorn sweatshirt again. I put on my pink leggings, and white socks and sneakers. And, of course, I wore my unicorn charm necklace. I was all ready for the Circus DeMarco.

Our seats were in a middle row. The tent was not too big, so we could see everything. Mommy bought Andrew and me some caramel popcorn and a drink. Then the lights went out and the circus began.

Andrew and I had already been to the circus, of course. But Mommy and Seth had

not. I was glad to see them smiling and happy. They had not been smiling much lately.

The show was the same as before. But it was still very exciting. I remembered when I went to circus camp, I had learned how to do some acrobatic tricks, how to juggle, and how to walk on a tightrope. They are all harder than they look.

I could not wait to see the unicorn again. I decided to make my last two wishes one more time, as soon as he came out, even though I would not be very close. Maybe I could try to get closer to him after the show. Was I being too pushy, making my wishes again? I was not sure. I just wanted Bob to hear me. The wishes were very important to my family.

Bob was the last act. The beautiful maiden led him into the ring. Magical sparkly glitter floated down from the tent roof. The spotlight made Bob gleam like sunshine on snow.

I tapped Mommy's hand. "Isn't he beautiful?"

"Yes, he certainly is," said Mommy.

Bob performed his act very well. Then the ringmaster asked for questions. This time I did not yell out anything. I did not need to ask if he was real, because I knew he was. Other people asked questions, and Bob answered yes or no. One boy asked which football team was going to win the game next weekend, but of course Bob could not answer that.

Then the maiden led the unicorn out of the ring. The lights came back on. The show was over. It had been wonderful, even though I had seen it before.

"That was lovely," said Mommy. "I am very glad we came."

"It was the best circus I have seen in a long time," said Seth.

"Maybe you could set up a circus tent in our yard," said Andrew. "A little one. Then you could have your workshop there."

Seth laughed and ruffled Andrew's hair.

"Thank you for the idea," he said. "It might be too cold in the winter, though."

"Oh. I did not think of that," said Andrew.

"Mommy, I need to see the unicorn up close again," I said. "Can we go to the other tent?"

"I am sorry, honey," said Mommy. "That was a special tour just for your school. We are not allowed to go there today."

"I really need to see him," I said.

"I am sorry, sweetie," said Mommy.

We shuffled forward with all the other people. Then I had an idea.

"Mommy, I need to use the rest room," I whispered.

"The lines are very long," said Mommy. "Can you wait till we get home?"

"No." I shook my head. "I really, really need to go now."

Outside were two portable toilets. One for boys and one for girls. Seth and Andrew got into the boys' line. (Andrew had to go too.) Mommy and I got into the girls' line. We

waited for a long time. The line was right next to the little tent where Bob's stall was. I kept trying to see into the tent, but the flaps were closed.

"Do you want to go first?" asked Mommy when it was our turn.

"No, you can go first," I told her.

"Okay. Please stay right here," said Mommy. "Do not go anywhere else. Do not take your hand off the door. It is very crowded, and I do not want to lose you."

"Okay," I said.

As soon as Mommy closed the little door, I stooped down and pulled up the edge of the tent. (I was not disobeying Mommy since I was still touching the door.) I got on my hands and knees and peered inside the tent. I saw Bob!

Is Bob Real?

Bob was with the beautiful maiden. (She was wearing another running suit.) Quickly I sent my wishes in his direction. He did not look over at me.

The maiden unbuckled Bob's fancy sequined circus costume. She lifted it off his back and hung it on a hook. Then she took off his sparkly bridle and hung that on another hook. Bob shook his head, as if he were glad it was gone.

Then the maiden took out a currycomb and ran it down his side. (A currycomb is a special comb just for horses. I know all about ponies and horses because I went to sleepaway pony camp last summer.) Bob seemed to like being groomed. He reached for a mouthful of fresh hay.

The maiden talked to Bob, but I could not hear what she was saying. She reached up to his forehead and put her hand around the base of his horn. The horn almost seemed to wobble!

I gasped. Quickly the maiden looked up and saw me. She did not seem angry. She took her hand down and shook her finger at me, but she was smiling.

"You should not be there," she called. "Our unicorn needs his rest." She reached out and stroked his horn. She scratched his forehead. The horn did not wobble at all. Bob ate another mouthful of hay.

"Karen! Karen," I heard Mommy say. She patted my back.

I crawled backward from under the tent flap.

"You should not be doing that," Mommy

said firmly. "It is your turn in the toilet. Please go quickly. Seth and Andrew are waiting."

"Mommy, I thought I saw — " I began. Then I stopped. What had I seen? I *thought* maybe the horn had wobbled a little bit. As if the maiden were about to . . . take it *off* somehow. But was she? Afterward it had looked as steady as ever. And I could not see how it was attached. Maybe Bob had nodded his head, and it had looked as if the horn were wobbling.

I just did not know.

"If you are going to go, go now," said Mommy. "Other people are waiting."

I stepped into the portable toilet.

"Thank you for taking us to the circus," said Andrew. We were in the backseat of the car, on our way home. "It was great. Maybe I will be in a circus when I grow up."

"Be sure to thank your father for the tickets," said Mommy. "You may call him when we get home."

"Okay," said Andrew. He started humming circus music under his breath.

I sat and looked out the window. I was still not sure what I had seen. The maiden had touched Bob's horn and scratched his forehead. His horn had not looked wobbly when she did that. Bob had still looked quite real. And three of my five wishes had come true.

I reached up to tap my charm necklace.

It was gone!

I felt all around my neck. I patted my sweatshirt, in case the necklace had fallen and gotten stuck in it. I checked my seat. I looked on the floor of the car.

"Boo and bullfrogs!" I said. "I have lost my charm necklace!"

What to Believe?

My necklace was gone for good. Mommy and Seth and Andrew helped me search the house, but we could not find it. I remembered wearing it to the circus. It must have fallen off there.

Losing my necklace seemed like a bad sign. I still believed in unicorns, but was Bob a unicorn? Or was he just a horse in disguise? How could I be sure? I could not take him to a stream and dip his horn into it. That was the only unicorn test I knew.

I did not tell anyone what I had seen (or

thought I had seen) at the circus. I did not feel like talking about it with anyone.

On Wednesday during library hour I returned my book about Princess Rosamund and her unicorn. I saw another book about unicorns, but I did not want to read it. Instead I checked out a book about Sally Ride, the first American woman in space.

Then I had an idea. Ms. Colman was the best, smartest, most gigundoly wonderful teacher in the world. I trusted her.

"Ms. Colman?" I said. (I remembered to use my *very* quiet indoors-in-the-library voice.) "Do you believe in unicorns?" I held my breath.

Ms. Colman put down the book she was reading. She tapped her finger against her chin. "Well, Karen," she said. "I have to say that I do not believe that unicorns truly exist today."

"Oh," I said. I looked down at my feet.

"However, there are many, many things that no one is sure about," she continued. "For example, dinosaurs. Two hundred

years ago, if you told someone that dinosaurs used to exist, they would not have believed you. But now we know for sure that they did exist. New things, new creatures, are discovered all the time. Just because there is no proof of something does not mean it absolutely cannot exist. Scientists are surprised all the time. That is one of the wonderful things about science. And it is one reason why life is exciting."

Ms. Colman smiled at me and patted my shoulder. "I think you need to make up your own mind about unicorns," she said. "The idea of unicorns is very beautiful and very special. You can decide for yourself."

I smiled back at Ms. Colman. "Thank you," I said. Now do you see why I think Ms. Colman is the most wonderful teacher ever?

I felt better after my talk with Ms. Colman. But I was still unsure. If Bob were not real, what would happen to my last two wishes? What would Seth and Mommy do?

Did this mean I had to worry about them all over again? What if Andrew never learned to ride that stupid bike? My family needed help.

That afternoon Andrew came into my room. He was wearing his bike-riding equipment. I did not feel like helping him. I had too much on my mind.

"Karen?" he said. "I am ready to try again."

"Andrew, you are only four going on five." I flopped back on my bed. "I really think you are too young to ride a two-wheeler. No one rides a two-wheeler until they are at least six."

Andrew frowned. "That is not true," he said. "I know I can do it. Please help me."

"Maybe next year you can try again." I turned my back on him.

Andrew was quiet for a minute. Then I heard him sniffle. I frowned into my pillow. I hoped he would go away.

"Karen," he said. "I know I can ride a bike. I *know* I can. You are my sister. You have to believe in me." He sniffled again.

I thought about what he said. Andrew and I were brother and sister forever. It was my job as a big sister to believe in him.

I rolled over. I sat up. I put my hand on his shoulder. He was wiping his eyes. "Andrew," I said, "today is the day. You are right. I can feel it. I feel that Bob has granted my wish, and that you will go out there and ride that bike. Are you ready?"

Andrew smiled and nodded. He sniffled up the last of his tears.

"Okay, then," I said. "Let's go out there and do it. Bob will help you. I know he will."

I decided then that I believed in Bob, no matter what. Just like I believed in Andrew.

16

Andrew's Ride

Outside it was a little chilly. Andrew was wearing a sweatshirt. I hoped it would help protect him. Lately he had been covered with scratches.

"Okay, now," I said. "Remember everything I told you. Pedal hard. Steer the front wheel. Keep to the sidewalk. Do not look back."

"Okay," said Andrew. He tightened the strap of his bike helmet. He looked very determined.

I held the bike while he climbed on. He put his feet on the pedals.

"I am ready," he said.

"Okay, then. You can do it. I believe in you."

Andrew looked at me and grinned, then faced forward and began pedaling. He stood up on the pedals to get going. I ran in back of him, holding the bike with both hands.

Soon he was going too fast for me to keep up with him. I let go. Andrew kept going! He was riding by himself! I put my hands over my mouth, waiting for him to crash. He passed the big oak tree. He passed the holly hedges on our neighbors' lawn (they always scratched a lot).

Still Andrew kept going! I could not believe it! He was almost halfway down the block, and he was *still* going! I was so proud of him. He had really done it: He was riding a two-wheeler. And he was only four going on five.

I ran after him. And I realized something: Another wish had come true. One of the big ones. Thank you, Bob!

I also realized something else: Andrew was not stopping.

"Andrew!" I shouted, running hard. "Do not cross the street! Stop! Stop!" We are not allowed to cross the street without permission. Mommy needs to know where we are when we are outside playing.

Andrew did not answer. He got to the corner of our block and swung the front wheel to turn. He made the turn! He wobbled a lot, but did not fall over. He rode on the grass for awhile, then got back on the sidewalk. I saw his face as he turned. He was white with fear, but he looked excited too.

"Andrew! Where are you going?" I yelled. I was out of breath from running, but I followed him around the corner.

"I cannot stop!" he yelled back. He did not turn to look at me. "I am scared to stop!"

Oh, no, I thought. We had never practiced stopping. (We had never needed to.) What were we going to do? Andrew could not keep riding forever.

"Just crash!" I shouted. "Crash onto someone's lawn!" That would be bad, but it would not be as bad as hitting a tree or a bush.

"I cannot!" he shouted back. "I am afraid!"

I ran and ran after him. Soon Andrew came to the end of the next block. It looked as if he were not going to turn! Uh-oh.

I glanced up and down the street. It was completely empty — no cars. Stay away, cars, I thought. I pounded down the sidewalk.

This time Andrew bumped over the curb and rode into the street. I held my breath. Streets are very, very dangerous. I am not allowed to ride my bicycle in the street. On the other side, Andrew rode up a low curb onto the sidewalk. I looked both ways again, then ran across the street myself. I was not supposed to do that, but I had to stay with Andrew, no matter what.

Now Andrew was riding down a very long, unbroken stretch of sidewalk. It was next to a huge lot that was covered with grass and weeds and some trash. There were no streets to cross for a long time.

"Pedal backward!" I called. My voice was hoarse from yelling. "Pedal backward to stop!"

"I am scared!" Andrew yelled.

I cupped my hands around my mouth. "Do it anyway!" I screamed as loudly as I could. "You have to stop!"

Suddenly Andrew stood up on his pedals and pushed backward. The bike instantly came to a hard stop, throwing Andrew over the handlebars. Then the bike wobbled and fell to its side.

"Andrew!" I ran as fast I could. Andrew was lying on the sidewalk. "Andrew, are you okay?"

When I reached him, I looked in his face. He blinked up at me, then grinned.

"I did it!" he said happily. "I rode a two-wheeler. For a long way, too!"

He sat up and we hugged each other.

"I knew you could do it," I said. "I knew it all along."

Where Are We?

I felt Andrew all over to check for broken bones. He did not seem to have any. But the front tire of the bike was flat. We found a small nail sticking out of it.

"Let's wheel the bike home," I said. "Mommy or Seth can fix the tire."

"Okay." Andrew looked around. "But where is home?"

I looked around too. This place did not look familiar. Mommy usually did not drive on this street. The abandoned lot was huge and empty. Across the street were some little houses and a mini-mall that I did not remember seeing before.

"We have not gone far," I said. "We turned one corner and crossed only one street. We just need to head back where we came from. When we get to our street, I will recognize it." I hope, I added to myself.

We decided to cross the street and walk next to the houses, instead of next to the empty lot. It seemed safer. We looked carefully both ways. No cars were coming. I wheeled the bike, and Andrew held one of my hands.

The little mall looked new. Several businesses were there. SILVER SHOES BALLET STUDIO, said one sign. A. E. CONKLIN, LOCKSMITH AND HARDWARE. Two stores were empty. Their windows were covered with white paper. A large sign said, NOW RENTING. CALL 555-8954.

"I wonder what will be there," said Andrew. "Maybe a toy store or a candy store."

"That would be fun," I said. "Or a bookstore. Or a video rental place. Or a pet store."

Empty store, empty store, I thought. It could be any kind of store. Or business.

I stopped suddenly in the middle of the sidewalk. "Andrew, those stores could be *anything*," I said.

"Yeah."

"Anything at *all*." I bounced on my heels. I had just gotten the most gigundoly fabulous, incredible, fantastic idea ever. I looked at the phone number again, and repeated it to myself over and over.

"Come on!" I cried. "We have to get home!"

We walked faster down the sidewalk. At the end of the block, our street was cally-corner to where we were standing. I looked down it, and we crossed the street turned diagonally. Now I knew exactly where we were. There was our house, where Mommy and Seth would be waiting.

"We will have to tell Mommy about crossing the street," Andrew said.

"I know," I replied. "But it was an accident. Maybe she will not be too mad. Maybe she will be so excited about your riding a two-wheeler that she will not mind too much."

"I hope so," said Andrew. "I really did it, didn't I?" He smiled happily.

"You sure did."

"I need to work on stopping," Andrew said with a frown.

"You sure do. I will help you practice."

When we got home, we put the bike in the garage. Mommy came out when she heard us open the door.

"There you two are," she said. "We were getting worried. Seth is already home. It is almost time for dinner."

"I am sorry we are late," I said. "But we have lots of wonderful news!"

The Little Store

After Andrew and I washed up for dinner, Andrew told Mommy and Seth about his bike ride.

"That is wonderful, sweetie," said Mommy. "But I am worried that you will really hurt yourself."

"I am a good bike rider," Andrew said. "I will practice stopping. Then you will not have to worry."

"I am proud of you, Andrew. You worked very hard at learning to ride a bike," said Seth. "I will fix your tire tomorrow. And it was very nice of Karen to spend so much time helping you learn."

I sat up straighter in my chair as everyone smiled at me. "It is my job as a big sister," I said.

"Now that you are riding a two-wheeler," said Mommy, "I want you to promise me that you will not cross a street again unless I am there. Do you understand?"

"Yes," said Andrew.

"And until you learn how to stop, you may not go around the block, okay?"

"Okay," said Andrew.

We sat down to eat our dinner. We were having a pot roast with potatoes, carrots, and celery. It is one of my favorite meals.

"I have more gigundoly wonderful news," I said.

"What is it?" asked Mommy.

"I have found Seth's new workshop!" I announced dramatically.

"Oh?" said Mommy.

"Yes." I told Mommy and Seth about the little mall I had seen on Andrew's bike ride.

I told them about the two empty stores. Finally, I told them the phone number to call.

"I am sure it will be perfect," I said. "Because today the unicorn granted my last two wishes. Andrew learned to ride a two-wheeler, and Seth has his new workshop."

Mommy and Seth smiled, but they still looked worried.

"It might not be as easy as that, Karen," said Seth. "But thank you for trying to help. I will call the number and ask about the space. But I think I have seen most of the places to rent in Stoneybrook, and there is nothing suitable. I really do not know what we are going to do."

I waved my hand. "Do not worry anymore," I said breezily. "The unicorn sent me to that store. I am sure of it. Our problems are over. You will see."

The Three Musketeers

During recess on Monday, the Three Musketeers grabbed three swings in a row. I told Hannie and Nancy about Andrew's learning to ride a two-wheeler.

"Wow," said Hannie. "And he is only four. I was almost seven when I learned."

"I was almost six," said Nancy.

"I taught him how myself," I said. "Just like I taught him how to read."

"He is lucky to have a big sister like you," said Hannie. She smiled at me. "Linny has taught me some things too." Linny is Hannie's big brother. He is nine.

"I do not have a big brother or sister," said Nancy. "I have to learn everything myself."

"But you will be able to teach Danny," I said. Danny is Nancy's baby brother.

Nancy smiled. "That is true."

"One of my unicorn wishes was that Andrew would learn how to ride his bike," I reminded my friends. "And it came true. And then that same day, I found Seth's new workshop. That was my last wish. Bob granted all my wishes. Now do you believe in him?"

Hannie lay on her stomach on the swing and twisted it around. Then she picked up her feet and let it spin her around.

"Well, no," she said finally. "I guess I still do not believe that Bob was a real unicorn. I am sorry, Karen. But I am very glad all your wishes came true."

"I think you made your wishes come true

by yourself," said Nancy. "You studied for your test. You wrote to Maxie. You told your mom that you wanted to see the circus again, so she said yes to your dad when he gave her the tickets. You practiced bike riding with Andrew a million times."

"What about Seth's workshop?" I said.

"That just happened," said Nancy.

"Sometimes things just happen," agreed Hannie. "And you do not know for sure if Seth will take that store."

I snorted. "I think Bob granted all my wishes. I have decided to believe in him."

"Okay," said Nancy. "It is all right if you believe in him."

"Yeah," said Hannie. "Anyway, even if Bob is not a real unicorn, that does not mean unicorns do not exist. We just do not know. Not really."

Nancy began to swing higher and higher. I did too.

I wished all of the Musketeers believed in unicorns. But I knew I could not *make* them believe. And they were very nice about my believing in unicorns. They would never tease me about it.

That is because we are best friends.

That afternoon I ran home from the school bus. It had gotten cooler during the day. I waved good-bye to Nancy and raced up the sidewalk to the little house.

Inside, the house was warm and cozy. I smelled cinnamon.

"Here I am," I yelled, dropping my books at the bottom of the stairs. "I am home! It is me, Karen!"

"I hear you," Mommy called. "We are in the kitchen."

Andrew was already drinking hot apple cider. He waved a cookie at me. "I told Miss Jewel that I could ride a two-wheeler. She could hardly believe it. I told her my big sister taught me." (Miss Jewel is Andrew's teacher. He adores her.)

I gave Andrew a smile. "This afternoon

you should practice stopping. You can stay in our driveway. I think you should stop at least five times."

"Okay," said Andrew.

We heard the front door open and then close. Mommy looked surprised.

"Seth?" she called.

Seth came into the kitchen. A big smile was on his face.

"You are home very early," said Mommy.

"That is right," said Seth. First he hugged Mommy. Then he hugged me. Then he hugged Andrew. I do not know why, but we all started laughing.

"What is it?" asked Mommy.

"I have gigundoly wonderful news," said Seth.

The Last Wish

"**W**hat? What? What?" I said. I started jumping up and down.

"Karen," said Mommy.

I quit jumping.

Seth took a bite of cookie. "This morning I went to look at the stores Karen and Andrew found."

"Yes," said Mommy. "You told me you were going to."

"I called the number and asked the real-estate agent to meet me there," said Seth.

"And? And?" I said.

"And it is . . . perfect! The store is a very good size — a little bit bigger than the space I have now. And the rent is pretty low, because the owners are eager to rent the space. It will be an excellent workshop. Best of all, it is only three blocks from home. I will be able to walk to work. And it will be better for you too, Lisa," he told Mommy. "You will be able to go back and forth between the shop and the house very easily."

"Oh, Seth, that sounds wonderful," said Mommy.

"Hooray!" said Andrew.

"Hooray!" I said. I lifted my glass of apple cider in a toast. "Here's to Bob," I said.

"Here's to Bob," said Mommy, Seth, and Andrew.

We decided to take a walk and see Seth's new workshop.

I was so happy about the workshop. Mommy and Seth were very happy about it too. I was glad we would not have to worry anymore. I was also glad I did not have to wonder about Bob. This proved it. He was real. All my wishes had come true.

"Oh, I am so glad this shop will work out," said Mommy.

"Me too," said Seth. "It will be terrific. And it is all thanks to Karen."

"And me," said Andrew. "If I had known how to stop, Karen would not have found the shop."

"That is true," said Seth.

I held Mommy's hand and kicked through little piles of red and gold and brown leaves on the ground.

We reached the mall. Seth was going to take the shop at the very end, because it had the most windows. He showed us where his name would be painted on the door. We peered through cracks in the white paper covering the windows. Inside it looked big and empty. But I could imagine it filled with Seth's wood and his tools. Then it would be very cheerful inside.

"I have an idea," said Seth. "Let's go out to dinner to celebrate."

"That is a wonderful idea," said Mommy. "Karen and Andrew can pick the place."

"Pizza!" Andrew and I said at the same time. We grinned at each other.

It was starting to get dark, and we headed for home. Just then I heard a loud rumbling, and turned around to see what it was. On the street by Seth's new workshop, a line of trucks was rolling slowly along.

"It is the circus!" I said. "I guess it is over and they are leaving town."

We stopped to watch it go by. I saw several big trucks full of equipment. CIRCUS DE-MARCO was painted on their sides. Next came the trailers and campers where the performers lived. Some of them were looking out of their windows. They waved to us, and we smiled and waved back.

At the very end, was a pickup truck pulling . . . a horse van.

"Bob!" I cried.

A small window was open at the front of the van. I could see part of Bob's white head and mane. He turned his head, and one

brown eye looked out at me. I squinted my eyes, but I could not see whether he had a horn. I just could not tell for sure. I thought I saw it, but the window was small, and . . .

Oh, Bob, I thought. Are you real? Are you?

And then (you will not believe this, but I promise it happened), Bob winked at me! He winked! He looked right at me and winked!

He had heard me wonder, and he had winked at me. I guess you know what that means.

I will never have to wonder about Bob again.

Hooray for unicorns!

About the Author

ANN M. MARTIN lives in New York City and loves animals, especially cats. She has two cats of her own, Gussie and Woody.

Other books by Ann M. Martin that you might enjoy are *Stage Fright*; *Me and Katie (the Pest)*; and the books in *The Baby-sitters Club* series.

Ann likes ice cream and *I Love Lucy*. And she has her own little sister, whose name is Jane.

Little Sister

Don't miss # 90

KAREN'S HAUNTED HOUSE

"Come on, Hannie," I said. "Let's get out of here."

Hannie and I were heading for the staircase when suddenly — "*A wooo, a wooo.*" A loud, scary, howling sound surrounded us! It sounded like a pack of wolves! I grabbed Hannie's hand. Her eyes were big. She looked about as scared as I felt. Then, *wham!* A door slammed down the hall. But no one was there!

"This house really *is* haunted!" I yelled.

Little Sister

by Ann M. Martin
author of The Baby-sitters Club®

More Titles... ➡

❏	MQ48231-9	#59	Karen's Leprechaun	$2.95
❏	MQ48305-6	#60	Karen's Pony	$2.95
❏	MQ48306-4	#61	Karen's Tattletale	$2.95
❏	MQ48307-2	#62	Karen's New Bike	$2.95
❏	MQ25996-2	#63	Karen's Movie	$2.95
❏	MQ25997-0	#64	Karen's Lemonade Stand	$2.95
❏	MQ25998-9	#65	Karen's Toys	$2.95
❏	MQ26279-3	#66	Karen's Monsters	$2.95
❏	MQ26024-3	#67	Karen's Turkey Day	$2.95
❏	MQ26025-1	#68	Karen's Angel	$2.95
❏	MQ26193-2	#69	Karen's Big Sister	$2.95
❏	MQ26280-7	#70	Karen's Grandad	$2.95
❏	MQ26194-0	#71	Karen's Island Adventure	$2.95
❏	MQ26195-9	#72	Karen's New Puppy	$2.95
❏	MQ26301-3	#73	Karen's Dinosaur	$2.95
❏	MQ26214-9	#74	Karen's Softball Mystery	$2.95
❏	MQ69183-X	#75	Karen's County Fair	$2.95
❏	MQ69184-8	#76	Karen's Magic Garden	$2.95
❏	MQ69185-6	#77	Karen's School Surprise	$2.99
❏	MQ69186-4	#78	Karen's Half Birthday	$2.99
❏	MQ69187-2	#79	Karen's Big Fight	$2.99
❏	MQ69188-0	#80	Karen's Christmas Tree	$2.99
❏	MQ69189-9	#81	Karen's Accident	$2.99
❏	MQ69190-2	#82	Karen's Secret Valentine	$3.50
❏	MQ69191-0	#83	Karen's Bunny	$3.50
❏	MQ69192-9	#84	Karen's Big Job	$3.50
❏	MQ69193-7	#85	Karen's Treasure	$3.50
❏	MQ69194-5	#86	Karen's Telephone Trouble	$3.50
❏	MQ06585-8	#87	Karen's Pony Camp	$3.50
❏	MQ06586-6	#88	Karen's Puppet Show	$3.50
❏	MQ06587-4	#89	Karen's Unicorn	$3.50
❏	MQ06588-2	#90	Karen's Haunted House	$3.50
❏	MQ55407-7		BSLS Jump Rope Pack	$5.99
❏	MQ73914-X		BSLS Playground Games Pack	$5.99
❏	MQ89735-7		BSLS Photo Scrapbook Book and Camera Pack	$9.99
❏	MQ47677-7		BSLS School Scrapbook	$2.95
❏	MQ43647-3		Karen's Wish Super Special #1	$3.25
❏	MQ44834-X		Karen's Plane Trip Super Special #2	$3.25
❏	MQ44827-7		Karen's Mystery Super Special #3	$3.25
❏	MQ45644-X		Karen, Hannie, and Nancy	
			The Three Musketeers Super Special #4	$2.95
❏	MQ45649-0		Karen's Baby Super Special #5	$3.50
❏	MQ46911-8		Karen's Campout Super Special #6	$3.25

Available wherever you buy books, or use this order form.

Scholastic Inc., P.O. Box 7502, Jefferson City, MO 65102

Please send me the books I have checked above. I am enclosing $_____
(please add $2.00 to cover shipping and handling). Send check or money order – no cash or C.O.Ds please.

Name_____Birthdate_____

Address_____

City_____State/Zip_____

Please allow four to six weeks for delivery. Offer good in U.S.A. only. Sorry, mail orders are not available to residents to Canada. Prices subject to change.   BSLS497